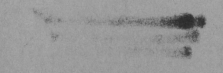

VISITING LANGSTON

VISITING LANGSTON

Willie Perdomo

illustrated by *Bryan Collier*

Henry Holt and Company · New York

To
Raymond R. Patterson
Blues bard
Poet maker
May you be singing
your *Elemental Blues*
in the heaven
of your choice.

      ——W. E. P.

I dedicate
this book to both
children and adults.
I point you all
to the artistry of
Langston Hughes
because in it there is a
mirror, a place for you.

      ——B. C.

Author's Note

LANGSTON HUGHES was born on February 1, 1902, in Joplin, Missouri. He said he wrote most of his poetry when he was sad and, judging by all the poems he wrote, he must have been sad a lot of the time. I think what made him sad was how people, especially people of color, were treated. If you asked him why he started writing he would say that it started when his grandmother used to sit him in her lap and tell him stories. Langston loved music, ice cream, theater, and people——people from all over the world. His first book of poems was called *The Weary Blues*. He went on to write novels, children's stories, lyrics for musicals, plays, short stories, newspaper columns, and anthologies, and he was always generous with his time. He died at the age of sixty-five on May 22, 1967.

Today I'm going to wear
My favorite pink blouse

I'm going with my daddy
To visit Langston's house

Langston

Langston

Langston Hughes

Wrote poems

Like jazz

Sang like love

Cried like blues

He sat by the window

Writing about his trips

Across the big sea

He could tell you

What Africa means to me

He can tell you why my

Dreams run wild

Why Daddy says I'm like

Langston's genius child

Langston lived in a brownstone

On Langston Hughes Place

There is a frame filled

With pictures of his

Smiling face

I love hip-hop

Hop-scotch

And double-dutch

But I don't like

Catch-n-kiss

Too much

Ask me where I'm from

I'll say Harlem world

Ask me who I am

I'll say I'm a Harlem girl

Today I'm going to wear

My favorite pink blouse

I'm going with my daddy

To visit Langston's house

Langston

Langston

I write poetry

Just like Langston Hughes

• Mother to Son • JUKE
BOX LOVE SONG • Motto • **LIFE IS**
FINE • *Theme for English B* • HARLEM
NIGHT CLUB • The Weary Blues • *Justice* •
Still Here • *Harlem (Dream Deferred)* • Cross •
FLATTED FIFTHS • *Hold Fast to Dreams* • Song for
a Dark Girl • AFRO-AMERICAN FRAGMENT • Dream
Variations • SONG FOR BILLIE HOLIDAY • One
Way Ticket • *Ballad of the Gypsy* • BE-BOP
BOYS • Quiet Girl • THE NEGRO
SPEAKS OF RIVERS •

Henry Holt and Company, LLC

Publishers since 1866

115 West 18th Street

New York, New York 10011

Henry Holt is a registered trademark of

Henry Holt and Company, LLC

Text copyright © 2002 by Willie Perdomo

Illustrations copyright © 2002 by Bryan Collier

Distributed in Canada by H. B. Fenn and Company Ltd.

Library of Congress Cataloging-in-Publication Data

Perdomo, Willie.

Visiting Langston / Willie Perdomo; illustrated by Bryan Collier

Summary: A poem to celebrate the African American poet, Langston Hughes, born on February 1, 1902.

1. Hughes, Langston, 1902–1967——Juvenile poetry. 2. African American poets——Juvenile poetry.

3. Children's poetry, American. 4. Poets——Juvenile poetry. [1. Hughes, Langston, 1902–1967——Poetry.

2. African Americans——Poetry. 3. American poetry.] 1. Collier, Bryan, ill. II. Title.

PS3566.E691216 V5 2002   811'.54——dc21   2001003537

ISBN 0-8050-6744-2 / First Edition——2002

The artist used watercolor and collage to create the illustrations for this book.

Designed by Martha Rago

Printed in the United States of America on acid-free paper. ∞

1 3 5 7 9 10 8 6 4 2